P9-CME-036

by mouse & frog

Deborah Freedman

VIKING

An Imprint of Penguin Group (USA)

One morning,

Mouse woke up especially early,
eager to write a brand-new story.

"Once upon a time," Mouse began,
*"in a quiet little home, Mouse woke up
early and set the table . . ."*

"For F-r-r-o-o-g-g!"

said Frog.

"Frog. I am busy today," said Mouse. "I'm writing a story. **Once. Upon a. Time.** *Mouse woke up early and set the table . . .*"

"*For **Frog!***" repeated Frog.

". . . *for **tea,**"* said Mouse.

"And cake!" added Frog.

"**May**-be," sighed Mouse.

"And the King liked cake," continued Frog,
"so he came too—"

"What?" said Mouse.
"There is no king in this story."

"... and the King said, 'Let there be ice cream!'
and **ta-da!** there was ice cream,
all elevendy-seven kinds he liked best—"

"Not inside—it's too **melty!**" said Mouse.

Frog kept going.
"And the king proclaimed,

'Cake and ice cream for **ALL!**'

. . . and so from all across the kingdom his loyal subjects smelled their most favorite good things to eat and they flew right over—"

"No **no NO!**"
Mouse moaned.

"...*a-a-a-a-a-a-a-and*"—
Frog took a deep breath—
"*some had two feet and some had four and some had a comb*
and a brush and a bowl full of chicken soup, with noodles,
not rice, and they cheered we are here! We are here! We
are here! We have no end of stinky cheese! And they played
bump-bump and tumble, and hey diddle diddle all-fall-down,
kuplink, kuplank, do you like my hat? You monkeys, you,
I do! I do! What would you do if your mother asked . . .
are you my mother? Have a carrot. Then they sat just quietly,
smelling ring-around-the-rosies, patty-
cake, patty-cake, frankooberry mush, but
the sky is falling! No more blue! May I
bring a friend? Can I drive the bus? I think
I can—I think I can—and millions and
billions and trillions flew over . . ."

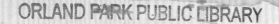

"This story is a **mess!**" cried Mouse.

"Mouse! That was not nice!"

"B-but . . ." said Mouse . . .

"once upon a time **Mouse** was trying
to tell a story, but Frog **bounced** and **bounced**
without listening to **Mouse!**"

"Oh," said Frog to Mouse.
"I just wanted to help."

Then Frog explained
to everyone else,
"This story is **Mouse's**."

scritch
Scritch
scratch

"So," Frog said,
"*Mouse set the table for tea.*
Then what happened?"

"Then," said Mouse, "Frog came over!
And they had cupcakes! And also played checkers."

Frog sighed. *"But Mouse didn't want any help."*

"Frog . . . ?

"What if, *then Mouse and Frog went to play outside?*
In a beautiful **garden**," Mouse said.

"Play **outside**?" said Frog.

"In a **magical** garden?
With a humongous beanstalk?
And a giant?
And **fee-fi-fo** . . ."

"Frog, not again!"
squeaked Mouse.

"Oops. Sorry," said Frog.

"It's all right," said Mouse, "because **this** story is **ours**."

"It is?" said Frog.

"Yes! What if, *Frog and Mouse opened the door . . .*"

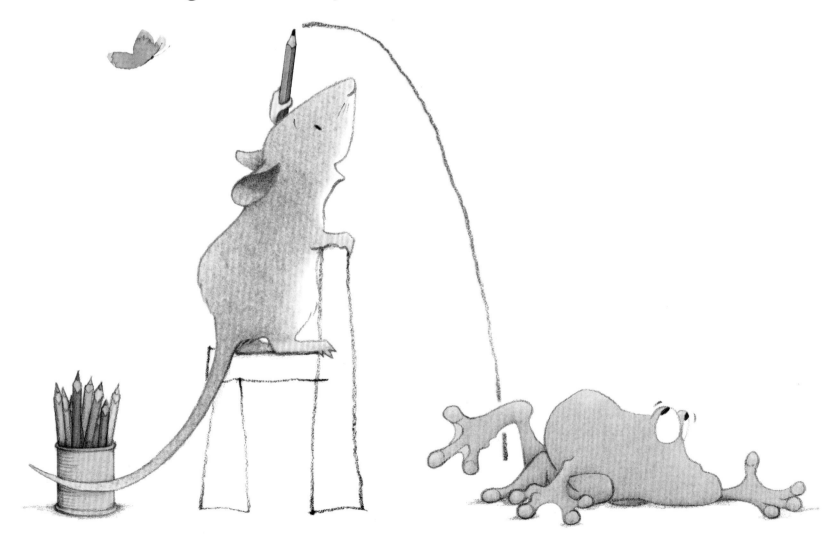

"*. . . and there were infinity-jillion butterflies!*" suggested Frog.

"Or just a **half**-jillion," requested Mouse.

"Can we have a fairy?" asked Frog.

"**May**-be," said Mouse. "Do fairies live in gardens?"

"If we want them to," said Frog.

"And Mouse, now is this story by Mouse **and** Frog?"

"Of course!" said Mouse.

"I like that, Mouse."

"Me too, Frog."

The End

for Aunt Mary Ann
and Uncle Norman

VIKING
Published by the Penguin Group
Penguin Group (USA) LLC
375 Hudson Street
New York, New York 10014

USA * Canada * UK * Ireland * Australia
New Zealand * India * South Africa * China

penguin.com
A Penguin Random House Company

First published in the United States of America by Viking, an imprint of Penguin Young Readers Group, 2015

Copyright © 2015 by Deborah Freedman

LIBRARY OF CONGRESS CATALOGING-IN-PUBLICATION DATA
Freedman, Deborah (Deborah Jane), date– author, illustrator.
By Mouse and Frog / by Deborah Freedman.
pages cm
Summary: "Mouse has one idea about what a book should be and how to tell a story. Frog has another. What happens when these two very different friends try to create a book together?"— Provided by publisher.
ISBN 978-0-670-78490-5 (hardcover)
[1. Authorship—Fiction. 2. Cooperativeness—Fiction. 3. Mice—Fiction. 4. Frogs—Fiction.] I. Title.
PZ7.F87276By 2015
[E]—dc23
2014003078

Manufactured in China

1 2 3 4 5 6 7 8 9 10

The illustrations were made with pencil, pastel, watercolor, and gouache, and assembled in Photoshop.
Edited by Kendra Levin   Designed by Jim Hoover